THE DARK REALM

NargA
the sea
monster

With special thanks to Cherith Baldry

To Adam Dawkins

www.beastquest.co.uk

ORCHARD BOOKS
338 Euston Road, London NW1 3BH
Orchard Books Australia
Level 17/207 Kent St, Sydney, NSW 2000

A Paperback Original
First published in Great Britain in 2008

Beast Quest is a registered trademark of Beast Quest Limited
Series created by Working Partners Limited, London

Text © Beast Quest Limited 2009
Cover and inside illustrations by Steve Sims © Orchard Books 2008

A CIP catalogue record for this book is available from
the British Library.

ISBN 978 1 40830 000 8

10

Printed in Great Britain by J F Print Ltd., Sparkford, Somerset

The paper and board used in this paperback are natural recyclable
products made from wood grown in sustainable forests. The
manufacturing processes conform to the environmental regulations
of the country of origin.

Orchard Books is a division of Hachette Children's Books,
an Hachette UK company.

www.hachette.co.uk

NARGA
THE SEA
MONSTER

BY ADAM BLADE

ORCHARD BOOKS

Welcome. You stand on the edge of darkness, at the gates of an awful land. This place is Gorgonia, the Dark Realm, where the sky is red, the water black and Malvel rules. Tom and Elenna – your hero and his companion – must travel here to complete the next Beast Quest.

Gorgonia is home to six of the deadliest Beasts imaginable – minotaur, winged stallion, sea monster, Gorgon hound, mighty mammoth and scorpion man. Nothing can prepare Tom and Elenna for what they are about to face. Their past victories mean nothing. Only strong hearts and determination will save them now.

Dare you follow Tom's path once more? I advise you to turn back. Heroes can be stubborn and adventures may beckon, but if you decide to stay with Tom, you must be brave and fearless. Anything less will mean certain doom.

Watch where you step...

Kerlo the Gatekeeper

PROLOGUE

Odora stood at the stern of the ship
and peered out across the Black Ocean
of Gorgonia. The only light came from
the purple moon, half-hidden by
cloud. She and her brother, Dako,
were trying to stay near to the coast,
but the dark night and the thickening
mist hid any land. There was no sign
of Malvel's guards. But Odora knew
that the evil wizard's men could be
prowling the sea and shore.

She glanced down at the huge chest of weapons near her feet. A surge of grim satisfaction shot through her as she thought about how these arms would help the Gorgonian rebels in their fight against Malvel. But the stakes were high. If the evil wizard caught them with the smuggled weapons, he would show no mercy.

Suddenly the ship lurched. Odora staggered forwards and saved herself from falling by grabbing the ship's rail. Her heart pounding, she hurried towards the bow of the ship, where she spotted the crouching figure of Dako.

"What's happening?" she whispered.

"I haven't seen anything," Dako replied in a low voice. "But we're not alone. There's something out there."

Odora clenched her hands to stop them shaking with fear. "We can't get caught. If Malvel's guards find the weapons we're carrying, they'll kill us!"

Dako shot her a warning look. "Keep your voice down. The rebels need these weapons. They're our only chance against Malvel." He peered cautiously over the rail.

"Can you see anything?" Odora asked, crouching low.

Before Dako could reply, a wave flooded over the deck, soaking them both. Then, out of the wave, rose a long, slender neck and a hideous, snake-like head. Terrified, the brother and sister stood rooted to the spot.

The Beast swooped down towards them, jaws agape. Odora leaped out of the way, catching a glimpse of rotten fangs and a flickering, forked tongue.

The vicious jaws grabbed her brother by the head and lifted him clear of the ship. Dako kicked out and pounded his fists against the Beast's scaly neck, but he couldn't free himself.

"Dako! Dako!" Odora screamed. She sprang up, reaching for her brother's legs, but he was already beyond her grasp. She saw his body go limp as the Beast vanished into the fog.

Behind her, Odora heard a second wave swirl over the deck and she spun round to see another head on a long neck rearing up out of the water. *Two Beasts!* she thought despairingly.

The second Beast stretched
out towards her, jaws snapping.
Odora dived away, sliding along the
soaking deck until she reached
the weapons chest. Throwing it
open, she pulled out a sword and
swung at the sea monster with all
her might. The Beast's head reared
away from her gleaming blade.

But five more heads appeared out
of the mist, joining the other Beast.
They surrounded the ship, looming
over it and snapping at Odora, their
fangs long and sharp. She struck
out with her sword again, but the
six heads were too fast for her.
They weaved to and fro, darting
between her sword strokes. Odora
felt her arms grow weaker and the
sword heavier.

Trying to dodge one of the heads,

Odora slipped on the wet deck.
As she struggled to recover her
balance, the ship was raised out
of the water. The deck tilted.
Swords, spears and crossbows
skidded across the wet planks
and fell into the sea.

The heads reared up as one, and
Odora gasped with terror as she saw
that all the necks extended out of
one huge, lumpy body. There
weren't six separate Beasts, but one
enormous Beast with six heads.
"No!" she screamed as the creature
wrapped its necks around the ship,
hurling it aside as easily as if it were
a pebble.

Odora was flung through the air.
I'm going to die, she thought in the
last seconds before she plunged into
the black waves. *And we've failed.*

Without the weapons the rebels have no chance of defeating Malvel. The Dark Wizard has won.

CHAPTER ONE

DECEIVED BY MALVEL

Tom took a short run, pushed off from the ground and soared into the air. Even though he wasn't wearing the golden armour, he had not lost its special powers.

But as Tom landed, pain stabbed through his leg. He looked down and saw that a sharp rock jutting up from the ground had torn through his trouser leg and cut his calf. He could have sworn that a moment ago there hadn't been any rocks ahead. But things were never quite as they seemed in Malvel's kingdom.

"What's the matter?" Elenna asked, riding up on Storm, with Silver, her wolf, loping alongside.

"I cut myself on a rock," Tom explained. "I'd better heal it before we go any further."

Tom removed his shield, which he carried over one shoulder. It held the six tokens he had won from each of the good Beasts of Avantia. Tom took out the talon of Epos the flame bird; it felt warm in his hand as he passed it across his bleeding calf. At once, the blood stopped flowing and Tom's skin drew together until there was no sign of a wound.

"Impressive," Elenna smiled.

As Tom replaced the talon, he felt a tingling in his shield. Sepron the sea serpent's tooth was vibrating again. The good Beast was being held captive by one of Malvel's evil Beasts, and Tom couldn't help but wonder what shape his enemy would take this time.

"Let's get moving," Tom urged, clenching his fists. "Sepron is still in trouble, and while there's blood in my veins, I won't let him die!"

Malvel had dragged the good Beasts into Gorgonia, leaving Avantia defenceless without its guardians. Tom knew that the Dark Wizard planned to send his own evil Beasts to conquer the peaceful kingdom.

"Let's have another look at the map," Elenna suggested, "and make sure that we're heading in the right direction."

Tom took the map out of Storm's saddlebag, shuddering as he unrolled it. Malvel had sent the map to Tom and Elenna when they first arrived in Gorgonia. Made from the skin of a dead animal, it smelled disgusting.

Elenna looked over Tom's shoulder as he traced a glowing green line that appeared on the map. It showed a route that passed through gentle-looking fields and ended at the Black Ocean, where a tiny picture of Sepron was now etched.

"At least the path ahead looks easier," Elenna said. "Fields all the way to the sea."

"Maybe this place isn't all bad," Tom said, shaking away thoughts of the next Beast he would have to face. "Let's go!" He stowed the map in the saddlebag again and strode out confidently along the track. Elenna urged Storm into motion and Silver bounded alongside.

As the day wore on, Tom found that the track didn't take them across fields, but wound upwards into craggy hills that grew steeper and rockier with every step. Storm picked his way carefully among the boulders, letting out whinnies of protest when sharp stones stabbed his hooves. Silver whined softly as he tried to find a flat spot to set down his paws.

"I don't understand this," Tom said, gazing around. "Have we come the wrong way?"

"This is the only way we could have come," Elenna replied. "The track didn't divide anywhere."

Shaking his head in confusion, Tom pulled out the map again. "Look," he said. "We should be on flat ground now. The map shows green fields."

Elenna looked bemused. "Why does it show fields if there aren't any?"

"Think about it for a second," Tom said, rage flooding through him as he realised what had happened. "Who gave us this map?"

"Malvel." Elenna's voice was tight with anger.

"Right," said Tom. "We must have been stupid to think we could ever trust it."

Elenna brought Storm to a halt. "We should stop," she suggested. "The map could be leading us in circles."

"There's one thing I do trust," said Tom. He dug deep into his pocket and pulled out the compass left to him by his father, Taladon. He held it in front of him, pointing it up the track.

Elenna leaned over Storm's head to look, and Silver darted around Tom's feet excitedly.

The compass needle was swirling backwards and forwards between *Destiny* and *Danger*.

"Does that mean we'll face both if we go this way?" Elenna asked.

"Yes, it does." Tom stowed the compass away again and straightened up, squaring his shoulders determinedly. "We'll keep going. We have to save Sepron – and ignore Malvel's tricks."

CHAPTER TWO

QUICKSAND!

The stony track grew steeper still.
Eventually it led between two sheer
cliffs. Tom walked Storm through
the narrow gap, and found himself
looking out across a wide plain.
He used his power of sharp sight,
which he had gained from the
magical golden helmet, and spotted
a glistening black line on the
distant horizon.

"I can see the Black Ocean!" he exclaimed, feeling renewed determination as he set eyes on the end of their journey. "We came the right way after all."

Elenna smiled with relief. "Then let's hurry. We need to get to Sepron as soon as we can."

The track wound down a rocky slope towards the plain. When they reached level ground, Elenna urged Storm to a trot and then to a canter. Tom ran ahead using the power of his magical leg armour, which gave him great speed. He felt certain that they would soon find Sepron and save him from Malvel's evil Beast.

Gradually clumps of grass began to appear, poking up through the thin soil that covered the plain. Here and there Tom noticed copses of twisted

trees, their branches thick with
drooping black leaves. He veered
away from them, remembering the
evil trees that had tried to capture
them on their Quest to find Tagus
the horse-man.

The ground under Tom's feet was
growing softer and soon he could see
clumps of reeds and pools of water
that reflected the scarlet sky. He

bounded forwards but gave a cry of alarm as he felt his feet sink into the ground.

Fear hit him like a punch in the stomach. "Stop!" he yelled to Elenna, who was cantering behind him on Storm. "Quicksand!"

Elenna pulled on the reins, but Tom's warning had come too late. Storm's speed carried him into the mire. The horse tossed his head and let out a neigh of terror as he began to sink. Silver skidded to a halt at the edge of the marsh, whining anxiously.

Tom used the power of the golden boots and sprang upwards, dragging his feet clear of the quicksand. While in midair, he grabbed Elenna by the shoulders and yanked her out of the saddle. They landed heavily on solid ground. Winded by the fall,

Tom sat up, hoping to see Storm pull himself free of the quicksand now that the weight of his passenger had been removed. Alarmingly, the brave stallion was still trapped and sinking quickly.

"I'm sorry, Tom!" Elenna gasped. "I couldn't stop him."

"We'll get him out," Tom reassured her. "Stay here with Silver and keep him safe."

Tom sprang up and ran to the edge of the swamp. Storm had sunk as far as his knees and was neighing in panic, trying to heave himself out.

"Don't struggle, boy!" Tom yelled. "Keep still! I'm coming to get you."

Tom thought fast and looked around. He had to find a way to get Storm out of the quicksand without falling in himself. Suddenly, he spotted a familiar figure near a copse of trees. He recognised the outline instantly. It was Kerlo, the Gorgonian gatekeeper.

"Kerlo!" Tom shouted. "Help us! Storm…"

He broke off as the gatekeeper raised one hand towards the branches of the tree before vanishing into thin air.

"Kerlo!" Tom yelled again in

frustration. Couldn't the gatekeeper see that Storm would die if they didn't help him? "He's useless!" he said bitterly.

"No, I get it!" Elenna shouted, running over to Tom. "Take your sword and cut some branches from the trees. Then we can set them down in front of Storm, like stepping stones."

"Yes!" Tom exclaimed. "I see now. Thanks, Elenna!" He drew his sword and dashed over to the trees. Quickly he hacked down some branches.

By the time Tom raced back with them, Elenna had taken out her bow and was tying a piece of long rope to one of her arrows.

"What's that for?" Tom asked.

"Watch."

Elenna fitted the arrow to her bow and fired it into the trunk of a tree on the other side of the mire. She picked up the end of the trailing rope and tied it around a dead tree trunk nearby, creating a tightrope across the quicksand. She repeated the process with a second arrow, but this time placed her shot higher, so that there were now two tightropes, one on top of the other.

"There," she said, giving both lengths of rope a quick tug to make sure they were secure. "Now you can walk along the bottom rope and drop the branches in front of Storm. If he doesn't stand on them for too long he should be able to get back over here. And if you need more support you can grab the top rope."

"That's brilliant!" Tom said with a smile. "I'm lucky to have such a clever friend with me on this Quest."

"Just hurry," Elenna said, her cheeks reddening.

Tom climbed onto the bottom rope and Elenna handed him the branches. He took his first step along the rope and almost lost his balance. He couldn't grab the top rope without letting go of the branches. His heart thumped as he stopped himself wobbling.

"Come on, you have to do this," he muttered to himself. He kept his eyes fixed on Storm as he pushed forwards along the rope. The brave stallion was floundering desperately and Tom could see him sinking deeper and deeper into the quicksand. Time was running out.

CHAPTER THREE

THE LAST STEP

Tom used the armful of branches for balance as he slowly walked out across the quicksand. He concentrated on putting each foot down on the tightrope, and soon he was moving at a good pace.

Eventually he reached Storm. The horse craned his neck up towards him as if he were begging for help.

"It'll be all right," Tom told him, dropping the first two branches in front of his friend. "Climb onto these and we'll soon have you out."

The sound of Tom's voice seemed to calm the stallion, but he didn't move towards the branches.

Tom stooped down as far as he dared without losing his balance on the rope. "Come on, boy." He forced his voice to sound soothing, even though his fear for Storm was rising. Soon the horse would be shoulder-deep in the thick black ooze, and if he sank that far, he would never get out. "Come on. The branches will hold you up."

Storm simply let out a frightened whinny.

"There's nothing for it," Tom muttered to himself. "I'll have to climb down and show him."

Carefully he lowered himself from the rope until he was standing with his feet apart on the branch nearest Storm. The surface of the quicksand quivered, but the branch bore his weight. Then he took a step forwards onto the second branch.

Storm's head went up and he blew a huge breath out through his nostrils. With a massive effort he pulled his forelegs out of the mud and stepped onto the first branch.

"Yes!" Tom gave a triumphant cry. "Come on, boy! You can do it."

He dropped another two branches onto the quicksand, then climbed back onto the rope and began edging along it. Storm had now managed to drag his hindquarters free and stood fully on the branches. Almost

immediately, the makeshift stepping stones started to sink, but Storm swiftly took a step onto the next one.

"It's working!" Tom called out to Elenna, keeping his eyes on the stallion's progress. She didn't reply, but he heard a loud bark from Silver and could well imagine the grey wolf racing back and forth excitedly along the edge of the mud.

As Tom dropped the last branch, he realised that the path he had made was too short and wouldn't get Storm to the edge of the quicksand. *I need more branches,* he thought. *But if I go to cut more, Storm will sink again.*

Tom drew his sword and slashed through the top rope. He grabbed one end and swung towards the bank, dropping his shield just in time for Storm to take his last step forwards.

Tom let go of the rope and landed neatly on solid ground, as Storm heaved himself up the bank and stood panting, his head down.

"Well done, boy!" Tom gave Storm a hug, not caring about the mud that plastered the stallion's coat. "Never scare me like that again."

Tom looked round to share his triumph with Elenna, but his friend and Silver were nowhere to be seen. "Elenna!" he called, darting forwards to rescue his shield from the quicksand before it was swallowed up. He scraped the shield clean on a clump of grass, gazing around as he did so.

Suddenly he spotted Elenna's bow and quiver of arrows lying abandoned on the ground. Fear gripped his heart. *She would never leave those behind*, he thought.

"Lay down your weapons," a gruff voice called out from a nearby thicket. "Or your friend gets it."

CHAPTER FOUR

WANTED ALIVE

Tom urged Storm to one side and grasped the hilt of his sword, ready for battle. A second later, the undergrowth parted and a group of men came out into the open. They wore ragged clothes and were carrying clubs, knives and swords.

Tom's stomach tightened with anger as he saw that their leader was gripping Elenna by the hair; in his other hand he brandished a long knife. One of the men held Silver by a rope. The wolf was yelping and snapping at his captor, but the man kept him at a distance with the use of a long club.

"I said, put down your weapons," the leader repeated.

Elenna twisted in his grip and kicked out backwards. "Get off me!" she yelled. "And leave Silver alone!"

With a cruel jerk the leader yanked on her hair and held the knife to her throat. "Keep still, you," he snarled.

Slowly Tom let go of his sword and lowered his shield to the ground. "Who are you and what do you want?" he asked.

The leader pushed Elenna forwards a pace or two. "My name's Jent. I'm a famous bounty hunter," he

boasted. "And these are my men."

"Famous? I've never heard of you,"
Tom retorted.

"You are not Gorgonian," Jent
sneered. "You and your friends are
intruders, and I'm looking forward
to the thousand pieces of gold that
Malvel has promised to the person
who captures you."

Tom stiffened. "What do you mean?"

45

Not letting go of the knife, Jent pulled a folded piece of parchment from his pocket and tossed it onto the ground at Tom's feet.

Tom picked up the parchment and unfolded it. Across the top, in large letters, were the words "WANTED ALIVE". Below this was a drawing of him and Elenna, with a caption that read: "These villains are guilty of intrusion, theft and treason."

Tom's throat tightened with fury. Malvel had made up these lies to stop him from completing his Quest. The evil wizard had obviously posted these parchments across the whole of Gorgonia. Clearly, Malvel was determined to set every member of Gorgonia against Tom and Elenna. They weren't safe anywhere.

"You can't trust Malvel," Tom said urgently to Jent.

The bounty hunter grinned, revealing a mouthful of black teeth. "I know full well who and what Malvel is. Why should I care? The only master I serve is money, and Malvel has plenty of that."

"You're stupid if you think Malvel will pay you," Elenna said bravely. "He'll cheat you – can't you see that?"

Jent ignored her and turned to his men. "We need to get to the town and send word to Malvel that we've captured these two villains." He nodded towards Tom. "Grab the boy; you can hurt him but don't kill him."

Silver suddenly let out a snarl, breaking free of the rope that held him captive. He lunged at the bounty hunter, but Jent was quicker and kicked him in the head. The wolf slumped to the ground. The slight rise and fall of Silver's sides showed that he was still breathing, but had been knocked unconscious.

"Silver!" Elenna shouted.

Rage surged through Tom. He grabbed his sword and ran towards Jent, but the bounty hunter's men stood in his way like a wall, their weapons raised.

As Tom struck out, Jent plunged back into the bushes, dragging Elenna with him. She struggled and kicked at her captor, but he was too strong for her.

A moment later Tom heard the sound of hooves and a horse burst out of the trees. Jent was in the saddle with Elenna held in front of him.

"Tom, help!" she cried. "Help me!"

As the horse raced away, Tom knew that his Quest to save Sepron would have to wait. First, he had to save Elenna.

CHAPTER FIVE

ON THE TRAIL

The Gorgonian bandits, careful to
stay out of range of Tom's sword,
formed a circle around him. "Make it
easy for yourself, boy," one of them
said. "Put the sword away."

"Make me!" Tom replied defiantly.
From some distance behind him,
Storm gave a whinny as if he were
cheering him on. Tom studied his

enemies. There were about fifteen of them, all muscular men with vicious weapons. Their smug faces told him they clearly assumed he couldn't possibly win against their numbers.

I'll show them how wrong they are, Tom thought.

As the first bandit stepped forwards, his huge club raised, Tom darted underneath his arm and gave the man a hard blow on the back with the flat of his sword. The bandit went sprawling to the ground. Tom spun round to meet his next attacker. As their swords clashed, the power of the golden gauntlets gave Tom unbeatable speed and skill. His sword flashed and, with a twist of the wrist, he sent the other man's sword flying, leaving him looking stupidly at his empty hand. As two more attackers

lurched towards him, Tom dodged between them, causing the men to crash into each other.

The bandits kept coming. One of them grabbed him from behind, and Tom drove his elbow into the man's chest. The bandit fell backwards, pulling Tom down to the ground with him. With screams of triumph, the others leaped on top of Tom and pinned him down.

Their weight pressed him into the mud and he thought he would choke on the stench of their unwashed bodies. Hands were grabbing at him from all directions.

"We've got him!" one of the bandits shouted.

Tom braced himself, summoning the superhuman strength that the golden breastplate gave him. He shot upright onto his feet, and the bandits let out yells of surprise and terror as they flew in all directions.

Tom looked about. The bandits lay sprawled on the ground. Some were stunned and not moving, while others groaned as they tried to get up.

To Tom's relief, Silver had recovered and was giving himself a shake. A low growl came from his throat when he looked at the bandits.

"Never mind them, boy," Tom said. "We've got to save Elenna."

He ran to Storm and leaped into the saddle. Urging the stallion forwards, he skirted the thicket and found the bandits' horses tied to branches on the other side. Tom took a moment to slash his sword through the reins and set them free. He slapped them on their rumps to send them galloping in the opposite direction from the swamp.

"The bandits won't be chasing us in a hurry," he said with satisfaction. Then he turned Storm's head in the direction that Jent had taken. Silver bounded alongside them.

Tom used the bounty hunter's trail of trampled grass and dislodged stones to follow him. It led away from the quicksand and the Black Ocean, back towards the mountains, but further east than the track Tom and Elenna had followed.

"I wish I knew this place better," Tom muttered to himself. "Jent said he was going to the town to get a message to Malvel, but I've no idea how far it is."

He thought of getting out the map again, but he knew he couldn't trust it. And it would be harder to spot Jent's trail once they reached the mountains. He had to catch up now. Tom urged Storm forwards.

At last Tom, Storm and Silver reached the mountains. The path wound among black rocks and Tom stiffened as he heard the sound of horses' hooves a little way ahead.

He leaned down and put a hand on

Silver's muzzle, signalling for him to be silent.

Slowing Storm to a walk, Tom followed the trail around a jutting boulder and spotted Jent some way ahead, riding up a long slope towards a ridge. Elenna was slung over the back of his saddle.

Tom urged Storm forwards again, hoping that the bounty hunter would not hear Storm's hooves on the rocky ground. Almost at once, though, Jent glanced over his shoulder and saw them. He dug his heels into his horse's flanks to pick up speed. A moment later he had vanished over the ridge.

Tom pursued him. Beyond the ridge was a steep slope covered with rocks, leading down into a narrow gorge. Jent was about halfway down, his horse weaving among the boulders.

"Stop!" Tom yelled. "Turn and fight!"

Jent glanced back at him, but he didn't stop or reply to Tom's challenge.

Tom was careful as he guided

Storm down the slope, but he still managed to shorten the distance between him and Jent by the time they reached the gorge. As the ground levelled out he urged the tired Storm into one last gallop.

Up ahead, Tom saw the bounty hunter draw his sword and scrape it against the rocky wall of the gorge before racing away.

"What's he doing?" Tom muttered. "Is he sharpening his sword so he can hurt Elenna?"

A rumble sounded from above Tom's head. Looking up, he understood what Jent had done. Vibrations from the bounty hunter's sword had dislodged stones from the rock wall, and they were now cascading down onto Tom and his friends.

Tom dragged on the reins and drew
Storm aside just as a huge boulder
landed inches from the stallion's
flying hooves. Then the roaring of
the rock avalanche was all around
them as they galloped forwards. Tom
ducked to avoid a rock and felt his
hair ruffle as it passed over his head.

Silver leaped over a rock which
thumped to the ground. A shower of
stones and earth knocked the wolf

over, but he scrambled up again and raced for the clear space ahead.

Leaning forwards on Storm's neck, Tom felt the patter of stone chips on his back and shoulders. His eyes stung from the dust and grit in the air.

Then he was through and the last stones of the avalanche were slamming down behind him. Jent and Elenna were nowhere to be seen.

Tom slowed Storm to a walk and looked carefully around. He examined the ground, but he still couldn't see anything to tell him where Jent had gone. Just ahead the gorge split into several different paths.

Which way? he thought desperately.

CHAPTER SIX

SILVER TO THE RESCUE

Silver suddenly let out an excited yelp. He darted forwards along one of the paths, sniffed the ground and looked back at Tom eagerly.

"Well done, Silver!" Tom cried, relief flooding over him. "You can smell Elenna's scent, can't you?"

Silver let out another yelp and ran on purposefully.

"That's right, boy, lead the way," Tom told him. "Don't worry, I'll be right behind you."

The path Silver had chosen led among rocks that gradually gave way to barren moorland. There was nothing to show Tom which way to go, but Silver, his nose to the ground, didn't hesitate.

The wolf led Tom to the top of a hill. Looking down, Tom saw a huddle of rooftops. Smoke rose from the chimneys.

It must be the town, Tom thought. He patted Storm's neck. "Let's go, boy."

The path led down the hill and into the town. Tom dismounted and walked beside Storm, with Silver on the horse's other side. The people in the streets gave them suspicious glances, but no one said anything.

The stench of Avantia had brought them trouble in one of the other towns of Gorgonia, but it seemed the smell was fading from Tom and his friends. No one sniffed the air now as they passed.

Tom noticed that the people were all hurrying in the same direction. He decided to stay with the crowd, hoping to overhear something about Jent and Elenna. He followed the locals into the town square.

A mass of people had gathered around a wooden platform in the centre. Tom had to force back a cry of shock and anger as he saw what was on the platform. Two sets of stocks had been set up. Elenna was trapped in one of them, her head and hands poking out of holes between the bars. Next to her, in the other stocks, was a girl with hair the colour of fire.

The crowd surged forwards as people tried to get closer to the platform. They jeered at the two girls and some were even throwing rocks. Tom saw one bounce off the stocks close to Elenna's head.

Tom looked down at Silver. The wolf's neck fur was bristling with fury. His mouth was drawn back in a snarl and a low growl came from his throat. Tom suddenly realised that Silver's anger could be used to their advantage.

He crouched down beside the grey wolf. "Go on, boy," he urged. "Get Elenna!"

At once Silver took off through the crowd. People scattered as he let out a ferocious howl, gnashing his sharp teeth. Men, women and children turned away from the platform, pushing and shoving each other as they tried to get out of his way.

Tom raced after Silver across the emptying square. He leaped onto the platform and dashed up to Elenna.

His friend's face was cut and bruised from the stones the crowd had thrown at her, but she gave Tom a weak smile. "What took you so long?" she asked.

"I had a bit of trouble with Jent's men," Tom explained. "But nothing I couldn't handle." He examined the heavy iron lock that was holding the bars of the stocks in place. "We've got to get you out of here," he said.

"Jent told me that the locks are enchanted. Only Malvel can unlock them," Elenna said worriedly.

Tom gave her a tight grin. "Too bad. We're not going to wait around here for him to arrive."

He drew his sword and focussed on the swordsmanship skills given to him by the golden gauntlets. Then he whirled his sword through the air and struck the lock. It shook, but didn't break. Tom struck again. Still nothing. Then, on the third stroke, the blade sheared through the heavy iron. The two parts of the lock dropped to the ground.

"Now the other one," Elenna gasped, as Tom lifted the top bar to free her. "We have to save Odora."

Tom looked at the red-haired girl trapped next to Elenna in the other set of stocks. Her face was bruised and white with exhaustion, but her eyes shone bravely. She watched intently as Tom struck at the second lock. It gave, and he tossed it aside.

"Thank you," she said gratefully.

Silver was standing on the edge of the platform, his head thrown back as he howled and howled. Tom realised that the threatening noise was keeping the townspeople out of the square.

"Make for Storm," Tom instructed Elenna, as he helped the two girls down from the platform. "We need to get out of here before the townspeople gather their wits."

Elenna and Odora staggered across the square to the corner where Storm stood, and Tom boosted them up onto the stallion's back. Silver leaped down from the platform and pelted across the square to join them.

The sound of furious shouting rose up behind them as the townspeople crowded back into the square.

"Stop!" someone yelled.

"Grab them!" another voice called angrily.

"Don't let them escape!"

Tom glanced back as he began to lead Storm away from them. He caught a glimpse of Jent, his face furious, struggling through the mob towards them.

We need to get out of here fast, Tom thought, wishing he knew the town better. *If the mob catches us, we're finished.*

CHAPTER SEVEN

NEWS OF NARGA

"This way!" Odora gasped, pointing down a side street. "We'll get to the edge of town faster, and there are woods where we can hide."

Relying on the speed given to him by his golden leg armour, Tom led Storm into the street. As the horse galloped between the rows of run-down houses, Tom could still hear shouts and the running footsteps of the townspeople chasing them. But Storm and Tom were fast enough to outrun their pursuers, and the sounds of the mob died away as they headed for the edge of town.

"What a pity!" Elenna laughed. "Jent will never get his thousand gold pieces now."

Once the town was behind them, the path led up a hill towards a wood. Tom loosened his sword in its sheath as he led Storm underneath the branches of the trees. He remembered again the evil forest that had tried to trap him and Elenna when they first arrived in Gorgonia.

The trees stayed still, though, as Tom and his friends plunged deeper into the woods.

Tom brought Storm to a halt in

a clearing. He helped Elenna and
Odora down. "Why don't you rest?"
he suggested. "I'm going to climb a
tree to see if we've been followed."

Elenna and Odora sank onto the
damp carpet of leaves. Silver flopped
down beside them, panting.

Tom used the power of his magic
boots and leaped right up into a tall
tree, where he could see past the hill
towards the town.

"There's no one on our trail," he announced, then turned to look in the other direction. His spirits lifted as he saw the glittering line of the Black Ocean on the horizon. Quickly he scrambled down and let himself drop beside Elenna and Odora.

"We've come a long way from the Black Ocean," he reported. "But if we get moving we should be able to get there before dusk."

"The Black Ocean?" Odora exclaimed. She stared at Tom, her eyes wide with fear. "That's an evil place. You mustn't go anywhere near it."

"Why not?" Elenna asked, sitting up, suddenly alert.

"There's something horrible lurking in the water." Odora began to tremble. "It killed my brother and it almost killed me."

Tom exchanged a glance with Elenna. Odora must have seen the next Beast they had to conquer.

He reached out to grip the girl's hand. "Tell us everything you know," he said. "It's very important. We are here to defeat the Beast who lives in the Black Ocean."

Odora looked uncertain, but after a pause she answered. "My brother Dako and I were part of a rebel force fighting Malvel. We were sailing up the coast with a cargo of smuggled weapons. We were almost home when an awful monster rose up out of the water."

"What was he like?" Elenna asked.

"He had a huge body and six heads." Odora swallowed. "He picked Dako out of our boat and I never saw my brother again." Elenna squeezed her shoulder comfortingly. "The monster capsized the boat," Odora went on. "I was thrown into the water and the next thing I knew I was washed up on the beach. Malvel's followers found me there, and I was too weak to run away. They would have killed me if you hadn't rescued me," she added. "I can't ever thank you enough."

"You are thanking us by telling us about the monster," Tom told her. "Can you remember anything else about him?"

"I heard Malvel's men talking about him," Odora replied. "They said his name is Narga."

"Did they say how he can be defeated?" Elenna asked.

Odora shook her head. "No one can defeat him. He's too powerful. Please don't even think of trying. He will kill you just as he killed Dako."

"We have to try," Tom said. He didn't have time to tell the young girl about his Quest, but he needed any help she could give him.

Odora drew a deep breath. "The rebels have another boat for emergencies. You are welcome to use it. We keep it covered with bracken in a cove just north of here. Look for a black pinnacle of rock shaped like a sword."

"Thank you," Elenna said.

Odora shook back her fiery hair. "Don't thank me. I owe you more than I can ever repay."

"Where will you go now?" Elenna asked her. "We can't leave you to be recaptured by Malvel's men."

"I'll be all right," Odora assured her.

"There's a rebel camp a few miles to the northwest. I'll be safe there. And so will you," she added. "We'll take you in."

"It might be hard for us to find you," Tom replied.

"We have a map that Malvel sent us," Elenna explained. "But we can't trust it."

"Let me see it," said Odora.

Tom fetched Malvel's map from Storm's saddlebag.

Odora unrolled the slimy scroll. "Here," she said, as she picked up a twig and scratched a cross on the map, not far from the coast. "There's our camp. You can't miss us." She gave Tom and Elenna a wry smile. "We're the friendly ones."

Odora rose to her feet, bade them farewell, and walked into the forest.

Tom watched her until she was out of sight. "I hope we meet her again one day," he murmured, helping Elenna to her feet.

"So do I," Elenna agreed. "She's brave and deserves to live in a better place than Malvel's kingdom."

Mention of the evil wizard made Tom straighten up determinedly. "So, are you ready to take on another Beast?" he asked.

Elenna set her hands on her hips. In spite of her cuts and bruises, her eyes were glowing with courage. "I'm always ready," she replied.

CHAPTER EIGHT

THE BLACK OCEAN

Tom and Elenna stood gazing out across the Black Ocean. Dark waves, edged with dirty scum, broke on the black sand of the beach. Tom had never seen such a dismal place.

Storm was pawing the sand restlessly as if he didn't like the feel of it under his hooves. Silver ran down to the water's edge, sniffed at the sea and backed away.

"Come here, boy!" Elenna called.

The wolf raced back up the beach and stood by her side, his fur spattered with black sand.

Elenna turned to Tom. "Can you see anything?"

Tom used his keen sight to look out across the calm surface of the ocean.

"I can't spot Narga," Tom said. "And there's no sign of Sepron, either." Anxiety stabbed at him as he wondered if they were too late to save the good Beast of Avantia.

"What do you think we should do?" Elenna asked.

Tom thought back to his first encounter with Sepron and when he battled Zepha the monster squid. His chest grew tight as he remembered the suffocating sensation of being underwater. "I want to keep this battle on the surface," he said at last. "It's too dangerous to dive, especially in this black water. I wouldn't be able to see a thing!"

"Then let's find the rebels' boat," Elenna decided.

"Yes, Odora said it was north of here," Tom replied. "Let's go."

Leading Storm, Tom and Elenna walked along the beach, keeping well away from the black water. Silver darted to and fro, snuffling at clumps of black seaweed and scum thrown up from the sea, whining uneasily all the while.

After walking north for some distance they came across a deep cove among the rocks.

"This looks like the place Odora told us about," said Elenna, pointing to a thin spire of stone at the side of the cove. "There's the black pinnacle shaped like a sword."

Tom left Storm on the beach and started scrambling over the rocks towards the inlet.

"Stay," Elenna said to Silver. "Warn us if you see anyone coming."

The grey wolf sat on the sand beside Storm, his tail slowly beating the ground and his muzzle raised alertly.

"It won't be easy to spot the boat," Elenna said, as she caught up with Tom. "Odora said the rebels had hidden it under some bracken."

Tom noticed that lots of the boulders around the cove were covered with dead, rust-coloured bracken. Then he spotted a heap of it lower down among the rocks, looking as if it were floating on the surface of the water.

"There!" he exclaimed.

Tom and Elenna clambered over the rocks at the edge of the water until they reached the floating bracken. Close up, they could see the wooden hull of a boat underneath it. They started grabbing the bracken in huge armfuls and tossing it into the water.

"We can't use it," Tom said, struggling with disappointment as he uncovered the mast, which was lying flat along the deck. "The mast is broken."

"No, it's not," Elenna explained with a wry smile. "It's supposed to do that. The rebels must have taken it down to make the boat easier to hide."

When they had cleared the bracken Elenna showed Tom how to hold the mast in place while she attached the bolts.

"It's a good thing I'm Questing with someone who knows the sea," Tom said with a grin.

Elenna checked the sails and the oars, and fixed the ropes in place. "The sails are a bit worn," she said, "but I think they'll do."

"I hope so," Tom replied. "We don't

know how far we have to go."

At last the boat was ready. Tom went back to Storm and Silver, and led the stallion carefully among the rocks until they reached some trees near the cove. He unsaddled Storm and gave him a farewell pat on his glossy black neck.

"We won't be long," he said. "You should be safe here."

"As safe here as anywhere," Elenna said, plunging her hands into the thick fur around Silver's neck and giving him a hug.

Leaving their friends hidden, Tom and Elenna climbed into the boat. Elenna used an oar to push it off the rocks, thrusting them out of the cove and into the open sea. Tom pulled on the ropes and the sails grew taut as the wind filled them. Elenna took the tiller and steered the boat out into the Black Ocean.

"Which way?" she asked.

"All we know is that Narga's lurking out there somewhere," Tom replied. He used his sharp sight to scan the water as the boat skimmed over the waves, leaving the land far behind. He started as something broke the surface not far from the boat, then relaxed as he realised it was only a dolphin. But when the creature surfaced again he realised it was not like the dolphins of Avantia. Light from the sky reflected red on its sleek black skin. Its snout was longer than an ordinary dolphin's, and when it opened its jaws it showed a set of sharp black teeth.

Tom shuddered. "The ocean is just as evil as the land," he said.

"I know." Elenna pointed into the water. "Look at that starfish. It has pincers just like a crab's."

Tom looked and caught a glimpse of gleaming black claws. From that point he decided to ignore the evil sea creatures and concentrate on spotting Sepron or the fearsome Narga.

When the coast was just a dark line on the horizon, Tom caught sight of something multicoloured drifting on the surface of the black water. "Over there!" he called, pointing.

Elenna adjusted the tiller and the boat tacked onto its new course. As they drew closer, Tom realised it was Sepron.

The noble sea serpent lay unmoving on the waves. His coils stretched out far across the surface, and the scales that had shimmered in the clear light of Avantia now looked dull and lifeless.

"I think he might be dead!" Elenna sobbed.

Tom didn't reply. He and Elenna both grabbed an oar and dug into the waves, trying to propel the boat even faster across the ocean.

"Sepron!" Tom shouted as they reached the great Beast.

But the sea serpent's eyes were closed and he didn't respond.

"Sepron, please wake up!" Elenna begged desperately, but the Beast's eyelids didn't even flicker.

Tom was torn between rage and despair. Had they come this far only to find that they were too late? He decided to use the power he had won when he defeated Torgor the minotaur – the power to hear the thoughts of the good Beasts of Avantia. Closing his eyes and opening his mind, he touched the minotaur's red jewel that was fixed to his belt. But he couldn't sense anything from Sepron.

"Tom," Elenna said. "Do you think—"

She broke off as a dark shadow loomed over them, cutting off the red light of Gorgonia's setting sun.

Tom whirled round. Rising out of the sea were six enormous snake heads.

"Narga!" Elenna gasped.

CHAPTER NINE

THE RAGE OF NARGA

"At last!" Tom exclaimed, drawing his sword. "I'll protect Sepron – or avenge him."

He sprang up, kicking his feet off the mast for greater height as he harnessed the power of the golden boots. Then he grabbed the top of the mast and, using his free hand, swung his sword at Narga.

The Beast's heads dodged the blow and darted forwards, snapping at Tom from all directions. He managed to evade them, but the gaping jaws were so close that he could see Narga's yellow fangs and smell his rotten breath.

Tom struck out again, this time aiming for the Beast's necks, but the monster was too fast. One of Narga's heads swooped down on Tom and jabbed his arm, forcing him to lose his grip on the mast and fall towards the deck.

"Tom – no!" Elenna cried out in alarm.

But Tom somersaulted neatly, landing nimbly on the deck beside his friend. She smiled in relief and raised her bow and arrow, ready to shoot. Tom turned to face Narga again, his

sword clutched firmly in his hand.
All six heads gave a roar of rage and
suddenly towered up towards the
swirling red sky of Gorgonia. Water
cascaded off Narga's back as he began
to rise out of the ocean. His body was
round and covered with glistening

black swellings, and reeking ocean mud dripped from his skin. Tom and Elenna watched in amazement as the Beast finally stopped his ascent and stood on the surface of the ocean. The six heads snarled and hissed, and then the evil Beast began to walk across the waves towards them.

"Now what do we do?" Elenna's bow and arrow quivered in her hand.

"We do what we always do," Tom replied grimly. "We fight!"

Before Narga could reach the boat, Tom leaped into the air again. Dodging the weaving necks, he landed on the Beast's back, slashing and swiping his sword at Narga's body, feeling the blade sink deep into his flesh. A couple of Elenna's arrows found their mark in the Beast's side.

The sea monster roared in fury and

jerked his body to and fro, trying to throw Tom off. Gritting his teeth, Tom struck the Beast again with all his strength. A violent spasm shuddered through Narga's body; then he was still.

"You did it, Tom!" Elenna's voice carried towards him on the wind. "You defeated the Beast."

Tom jumped back into the boat and turned, expecting to see Narga sink beneath the waves, but to his dismay the Beast's necks suddenly began to writhe and the snake heads let out a roar. Narga was not defeated; in fact, he seemed as strong as ever.

"He's still coming!" Elenna groped for an arrow.

Narga's six heads loomed over the boat once more. Tom raised his shield. Then, out of the corner of his eye, he spotted movement in the deep, dark water.

"It's Sepron!" Elenna gasped. "He's alive after all!"

Sepron's coils were flexing strongly, propelling him towards the boat. Close up, Tom could see cuts and gashes all over the sea serpent's scaly body. Tom's anger rushed up again as he imagined how the evil Narga had caused the injuries.

The great sea serpent thrust himself between Narga and the boat, and jabbed his huge head at the evil Beast. Narga stumbled back, although he was quick to recover himself. Fear stabbed through Tom as he saw all six of Narga's heads swoop down upon the noble Beast of Avantia.

The heads swarmed all over Sepron's battered body, snapping

and biting. The sea serpent let out a
bellow of rage and pain.

"Oh, Sepron!" Elenna's voice was
filled with despair.

For a moment Tom felt helpless.
Was this how his Quest was doomed
to end?

CHAPTER TEN

THE WHIRLPOOL

"I will not let Sepron die!" Tom clenched his fists.

"Then we need a new plan – and fast," Elenna replied.

Tom looked around him. Just a few paces away he saw a length of rope. Suddenly he remembered how Elenna had skilfully fired two lengths across the quicksand.

He leaped forwards and grabbed the rope. "Tie this to an arrow," he said, passing it to Elenna. "I need you to shoot it."

Elenna gave him a puzzled glance, but didn't hesitate. Grasping one end of the rope, she fastened it securely to an arrow.

"Fire when I give you the signal," Tom instructed. "Aim just past Narga."

Looking even more puzzled, Elenna fixed her arrow in place. Tom braced himself, preparing for the jump of his life.

Sepron lay limply on the surface of the water, though the feeble movement of his coils told Tom he was still alive. All six of Narga's heads let out a roar of triumph as they reared up to deliver another assault upon the good Beast.

"Now!" Tom exclaimed.

As Elenna loosed the arrow, Tom launched himself into the air after it. He grasped the shaft and directed it in a wide arc around Narga's necks. Touching down briefly on the Beast's back, he pushed off again, using the power of the golden boots, and landed back on deck at Elenna's side. All six of the Beast's necks were caught in the loop.

His friend was gazing at him in admiration. "Tom, that's brilliant!" she exclaimed.

Drawing on the strength of the golden breastplate, Tom grasped the other end of the rope and pulled it tight. Narga's heads thrashed back and forth, hissing with rage, but the evil Beast couldn't escape.

"Here." Tom thrust both ends of the rope into Elenna's hands. "Hold on!"

Elenna braced herself against the mast, her feet apart to keep her balance, as the furious Narga tried to drag himself free.

Tom drew his sword and whirled it around his head. When he let go, it spun towards Narga, and the sword blade sheared through all six of the Beast's necks. The sword curved round and returned straight into Tom's hand, while Narga's six heads dropped like stones into the Black Ocean and sank. Narga's body melted like butter on a hot day, until finally it dissolved into the water and was gone.

Elenna dropped the rope and let out a long, shuddering sigh. "You did it!" she breathed.

"We did it," Tom replied.

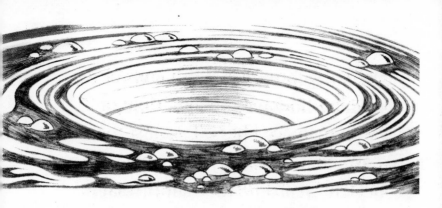

The place where Narga's body had
disappeared suddenly began to
bubble, then it swirled faster and
faster until it formed a whirlpool.
Tom and Elenna's boat was swept to
the edge of it but no further. Looking
down into the depths of the pool,
Tom saw sunlit green water, with a
sandy beach and gently rolling hills
in the distance.

"It's Avantia," he whispered.
"A gateway back."

Tom turned to look for Sepron,
who was floating on the waves a
little distance away from them. The
sea serpent looked exhausted from

the struggle and Tom felt a wave of pride at how well the good Beast had fought.

Touching the red jewel in his belt, he sent Sepron a thought message: *Sepron, come and see! This is the way home.*

The good Beast swam slowly to the edge of the whirlpool. He raised his head and stared straight at Tom and Elenna. Tom smiled warmly as he knew that the sea serpent was thanking them.

"Sepron is saying thank you, Elenna," Tom said.

"You're welcome, Sepron," Elenna replied, as the good Beast stared down into the whirlpool and then plunged into its depths.

Tom gazed after him and saw his many-coloured scales flare into life as he reached the sunlit water of Avantia. The sea serpent swam through the waves with all of his old strength restored. Then the sunlight began to fade and the swirling water grew quiet, until the boat was rocking gently on the waves of the Black Ocean.

"I wish we could go back with him," Tom said softly. "But we have a Quest to finish."

"Yes, we do," Elenna said with determination. She moved towards the stern of the boat and took the tiller. "Let's get back to the shore."

Tom grabbed the rope to tighten the sail, but as he did so he spotted one of Narga's yellow teeth floating on the surface of the ocean near the boat. A sparkling yellow jewel was embedded within it.

Tom leaned out of the boat and
fished the floating tooth from the
water, then used the tip of his sword
to work the jewel free. He slipped the
yellow jewel into one of the notches
on his belt.

"What does it do?" Elenna asked
eagerly.

"I don't know yet," Tom replied.
"I don't feel any different. Maybe it's
because I can't stop thinking about

the battle with Narga."

Suddenly his mind was flooded with pictures of the struggle. He remembered clinging to the mast while Narga's heads snapped at him. He recalled leaping onto the Beast's back and how disgusting it had smelled. He imagined that he could still feel the wind whipping through his hair as he leaped for Elenna's arrow.

"Hey!" he exclaimed. "I remember everything about the battle. The detail is amazing. I think the yellow jewel must give me a really good memory."

Elenna laughed delightedly. "That'll be a big help. Now we won't just have to rely on Malvel's lying map – we'll have your memory as well!"

Smiling, Tom took hold of the ship's rigging and the wind filled the sails, driving the boat back towards the shore of Gorgonia. However, before they had gone far, a familiar blue glow appeared in front of them, floating across the waves towards the boat.

"I think it must be Wizard Aduro!" Elenna exclaimed.

Even as she finished her words, the good wizard's form appeared.

Aduro was smiling. "Well done!" he said. "Tom, you're just as much of a hero as I always said you would be. As are you, Elenna."

Tom felt a tingle of pride. "We only did what we had to. We couldn't leave Sepron to suffer."

"What will the next Beast be?" Elenna asked.

The good wizard's smile faded. "I know your courage and your skill," he replied, "and you will need them both for your next Beast. You must be careful. You are about to meet Kaymon, and she is more evil than you can possibly imagine."

Tom exchanged a determined glance with Elenna. "Can you tell us anything else about her?" he asked.

But Wizard Aduro's form was already beginning to fade. His mouth moved, as if he was still speaking, but Tom couldn't hear the words.

"Wait!" Tom cried urgently, but the blue light had vanished. Tom couldn't see anything except the black waves and the rapidly approaching shoreline.

"I wish Aduro had been able to stay just a bit longer," Elenna said. "He always reminds me of home."

"I know." Tom was bruised and

tired, but nothing could destroy his determination to save the good Beasts of Avantia. "Remember, we're on this Quest to ensure the safety of our home. We'll face Kaymon, and whatever evil powers she has."

"And we'll win, too," Elenna agreed. "We've defeated three Beasts already."

"Which means we only have three to go!" Tom said. "We are halfway through our Quest – and while there's blood in my veins, we will succeed!"

Join Tom on the next stage
of the Beast Quest

Meet

KAYMON
THE GORGON
HOUND

Can Tom free the good Beasts from
the Dark Realm?

PROLOGUE

The night was dark as the injured rebel limped away from the castle on the moor. He had used a smuggled metal file to saw through his manacles, and the jagged-toothed edge had slipped and cut into his skin. The pain in his ankle burned, but he was desperate to get away from that terrible place.

He thought of his fellow rebels languishing in the castle dungeons. Many of them had planned to escape with him, but it seemed he had been the only one to make it over the drawbridge. He threw himself under a gorse bush, gasping for breath.

"I need to rest," he muttered to himself.

After a while he crawled out and cautiously lifted his head. He frowned. A thick grey fog was sweeping across the moor like a ghostly tide, drowning the hills and valleys. The fog would make it harder for the soldiers to find him. But it would also make it difficult for him to see the prearranged signal lights of the rebels' friends.

The man stood up, staring blindly into the

fog. Where were the lights?

Wait! He narrowed his eyes, peering into the distance. Then his heart leaped. He could see two yellow dots of light, blurred by the fog. The signal!

He stumbled forwards on his bleeding feet. Rescue was near. The lights were growing larger now, as if the bearers of lanterns were moving towards him. Two men, he assumed, walking side by side.

"Freedom or death!" he called. It was the agreed password.

He paused, listening for the response. But all he heard was a low moan that echoed through the fog.

He shivered, frowning again. Then he called the password once more.

The two lights began moving swiftly towards him. But although they rose and fell in a strange loping manner, they always kept exactly the same distance apart. A second low moan rumbled through the fog, and this time there was another noise – the unmistakable sound of large teeth snapping.

Suddenly, something huge came hurtling

towards him out of the fog.

The man let out a cry, throwing up his arms to protect his face. Through his fingers, he saw the salivating fangs and ferocious yellow eyes of an enormous hound. The lights he'd seen were the Beast's glowing eyes!

A moment later, the snarling creature was upon him, throwing him onto his back, its savage claws ripping at his chest and face...

CHAPTER ONE

DEADLY FLOWERS

Tom and Elenna stood in the prow of their boat as they returned to the shore of the Black Ocean. With the defeat of Narga the sea monster, another good Beast of Avantia had been freed – Sepron the sea serpent. The two friends leaped down onto the shingle, eager to be reunited with their animal companions. Silver the wolf let out a howl of delight, and Storm, Tom's black stallion, reared up, neighing triumphantly.

Tom and Elenna already knew that another Quest lay ahead. Wizard Aduro, their friend and mentor, had briefly appeared on the ocean waves, warning them that they would soon face another evil Beast: Kaymon. But he hadn't given them any more details.

Tom touched the blue jewel from Narga's tooth, which he had won in his last fight against the sea monster. He had placed it in his magic belt next to the red jewel, which gave him the ability to understand the good Beasts, and the green jewel with its power to heal broken bones. This new jewel gave him a knife-sharp memory. When he touched it, he remembered all the battles he had won in his Quest to rid Avantia of the Dark Wizard Malvel.

"Tom, look!" said Elenna. Tom turned and saw that his companion was studying the greasy, foul-smelling map of Gorgonia that Malvel had given them. She was pointing to a tiny picture of Nanook the snow monster which had appeared on the map.

Tom felt a sharp tingling in his shield. The bell of the snow monster, embedded there with the tokens of the other five good Beasts, was quivering.

Tom looked back at the map and the little image of Nanook. "Don't worry, my friend," he said. "We'll save you!"

"It looks as though she's being held captive somewhere in the south of Gorgonia," Elenna said. "But what kind of Beast could take her prisoner? She's one of the strongest of the good Beasts."

"Aduro said Kaymon was more evil than we could possibly imagine," Tom warned her.

"But what can that mean?" Elenna wondered.

"I think it's time we found out," Tom replied. The thought of Nanook being held prisoner burned his heart. "Come on, Storm – we have work to do!"

He leaped into the saddle and extended an arm to help Elenna up behind him.

"To the south!" Tom cried. "Let's rescue Nanook!"

The noble stallion galloped beneath the seething red Gorgonian skies, Silver at his side. Tom shivered, looking up at the red clouds that rolled and swirled above their heads. He would never get used to this terrible land!

"Don't forget to avoid the quicksand we wandered into before," Elenna said.

Tom nodded. "I remember it perfectly," he told her. "In fact, I can remember every hill and valley of this part of Gorgonia, thanks to Narga's jewel."

"That's good," Elenna said. "Especially as we can't completely trust Malvel's map.

Remember the trouble it got us into last time?"

Soon the Black Ocean was far behind them and the sun was low on the horizon. They entered a grim landscape of broken hills.

"Have you noticed it's getting much hotter?" Tom said, wiping sweat from his forehead. "It must be terrible for Nanook to be imprisoned here." The snow monster was used to Avantia's northern ice fields, her thick white fur protecting her from bitter winter winds.

As they reached the top of the first hill, they found themselves staring into a wide valley filled with gigantic bluebells.

"Oh, how beautiful!" Elenna said. "I would never have expected to find such lovely flowers in a place like this." She frowned. "But what's that shape in the middle? I can't make it out."

Tom peered across the valley. Although the precious suit of golden armour had been returned to Avantia, he still possessed its magical powers, and the armour's helmet allowed him to see far into the distance.

"It's Nanook!" he said. "The poor Beast is chained to a rock!"

Although shackled to a huge lump of amber, Nanook still looked majestic, her thick white fur glowing under the red clouds. But she was wrenching and tearing at the chain, clearly in great distress.

"That's so cruel!" cried Elenna. "How could anyone cause her so much pain?" She leaped from the saddle and began to run down the hillside. Silver bounded beside her as she headed towards the blue sea of flowers.

"Be careful!" Tom called, urging Storm down the slope after them.

He wasn't at all sure about the huge flowers, which had turned towards Elenna, almost as if they knew she was approaching.

"Wait!" Tom shouted, as Elenna and Silver waded into the waist-high stems.

A moment later Elenna stopped and began beating at the flowers with her hands.

"Tom! Help!" she shouted.

At her side, Silver was leaping back and forth, howling and snarling as though he were being attacked by an invisible enemy.

Tom could see what was happening. The dark red stamens of the flowers were stabbing like daggers, hemming Elenna and Silver in with their needle-sharp blades. Silver was yelping in pain.

"Ouch!" Elenna cried. "Tom – it's so painful."

Tom pulled on the reins and brought Storm to a halt. He swung down from the saddle. There was only one thing he could do. Gripping his shield, Tom drew his sword and swung his blade through the vicious flowers, cutting a path towards his friends.

The flowers stabbed at him as he hacked through. He felt pain as sharp as wasp stings as he sliced into the stems. Using the speed given to him by the golden leg armour, he quickly reached Elenna and the wolf.

"Come on!" Tom called, alarmed to see that the bluebells were swarming behind him, lunging forwards to fill the gap that he had made.

Elenna and Silver raced along with Tom close behind. The bluebells writhed all around them, striking at them like snakes. At last they came diving out of the flowers, skidding in the dust as they reached safety.

Tom stared out over the bluebells. Nanook

was still in the centre of the flowers, looking towards him in desperation. She lifted her arms and rattled her chain in anguish.

"The evil flowers are all around her," Tom said. "How will we ever be able to reach her?"

Then a low, mournful howl came echoing across the valley.

Tom and Elenna looked at one another.

"What was that?" Elenna asked.

Tom gripped his sword firmly. "Kaymon!" he said.

Follow this Quest to the end in KAYMON THE GORGON HOUND.

Win an exclusive
Beast Quest T-shirt and goody bag!

In every Beast Quest book the Beast Quest logo is hidden in one of the pictures. Find the logos in book 13 to book 18 and make a note of which pages they appear on. Send the six page numbers to us. Each month we will draw one winner to receive a Beast Quest T-shirt and goody bag.

Send your entry on a postcard listing the title of this book and the winning page number to:

THE BEAST QUEST COMPETITION:
NARGA THE SEA MONSTER
Orchard Books
338 Euston Road, London NW1 3BH
Australian readers should email:
childrens.books@hachette.com.au

New Zealand readers should write to:
Beast Quest Competition
4 Whetu Place, Mairangi Bay, Auckland, NZ
or email: childrensbooks@hachette.co.nz

Only one entry per child.
Final draw: 31 October 2011

You can also enter this competition
via the Beast Quest website: www.beastquest.co.uk

Fight the Beasts,
Fear the Magic

www.beastquest.co.uk

Have you checked out the all-new Beast Quest website?
It's the place to go for games, downloads, activities,
sneak previews and lots of fun!

You can read all about your favourite Beast Quest
monsters, download free screensavers and desktop
wallpapers for your computer, and send
beastly e-cards to your friends.

Sign up to the newsletter at www.beastquest.co.uk
to receive exclusive extra content and the opportunity
to enter special members-only competitions. It's the best
place to go for up-to-date info on all the Beast Quest
books, including the next exciting series,
which features six brand new Beasts.

Series 1

Ferno the Fire Dragon	978 1 84616 483 5
Sepron the Sea Serpent	978 1 84616 482 8
Arcta the Mountain Giant	978 1 84616 484 2
Tagus the Horse-Man	978 1 84616 486 6
Nanook the Snow Monster	978 1 84616 485 9
Epos the Flame Bird	978 1 84616 487 3

Vedra & Krimon: Twin Beasts of Avantia	978 1 84616 951 9

Series 2: The Golden Armour

Zepha the Monster Squid	978 1 84616 988 5
Claw the Giant Monkey	978 1 84616 989 2
Soltra the Stone Charmer	978 1 84616 990 8
Vipero the Snake Man	978 1 84616 991 5
Arachnid the King of Spiders	978 1 84616 992 2
Trillion the Three-Headed Lion	978 1 84616 993 9

Spiros the Ghost Phoenix	978 1 84616 994 6

Series 3: The Dark Realm

Torgor the Minotaur	978 1 84616 997 7
Skor the Winged Stallion	978 1 84616 998 4
Narga the Sea Monster	978 1 40830 000 8
Kaymon the Gorgon Hound	978 1 40830 001 5
Tusk the Mighty Mammoth	978 1 40830 002 2
Sting the Scorpion Man	978 1 40830 003 9

All priced at £4.99

Vedra & Krimon: Twin Beasts of Avantia and *Spiros the Ghost Phoenix* are priced at £5.99

The Beast Quest books are available from all good
bookshops, or can be ordered direct from the publisher:
Orchard Books, PO BOX 29, Douglas IM99 1BQ.
Credit card orders please telephone 01624 836000
or fax 01624 837033 or visit our website: www.orchardbooks.co.uk
or e-mail: bookshop@enterprise.net for details.

To order please quote title, author
and ISBN and your full name and address.
Cheques and postal orders should be made payable to 'Bookpost plc.'
Postage and packing is FREE within the UK
(overseas customers should add £2.00 per book).

Prices and availability are subject to change.